Mole's Hill a woodland tale

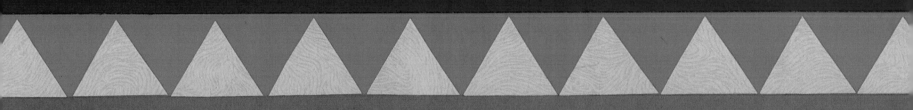

Lois Ehlert

Voyager Books
Harcourt, Inc.
Orlando Austin New York
San Diego London

Mole's Hill
a woodland tale

It was dark in the woods, but not everyone was sleeping. The stars were out. So was Fox.

Scratch, scratch, scratch.
Fox knew that sound.
It was Mole, digging a tunnel.
"Another hump of dirt!" snarled Fox.
"Where there's a mole, there's a mess."

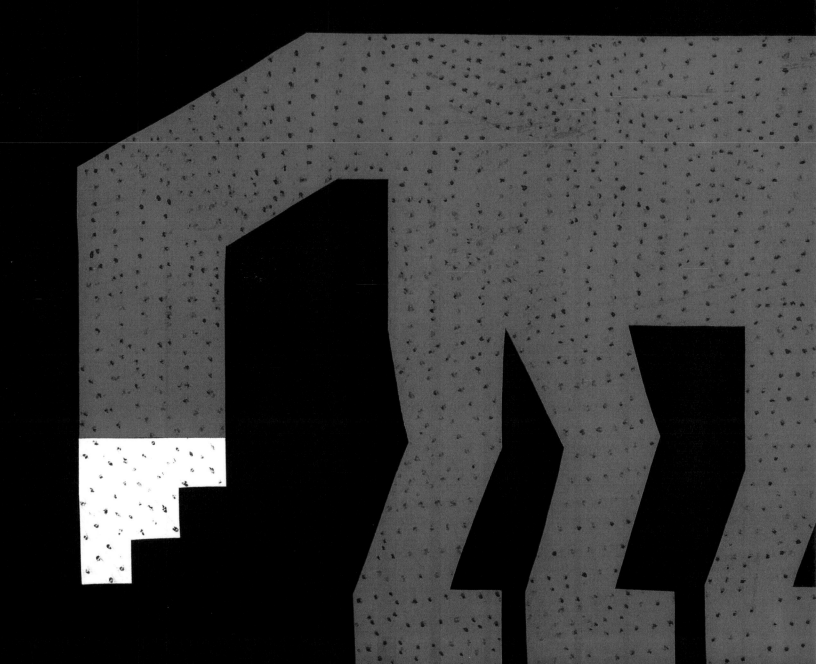

Digging tunnels was what Mole did best,
always on the lookout for a juicy worm for breakfast.
But once in a while she took a break and popped outside.

That's when she
found the note.

Mole

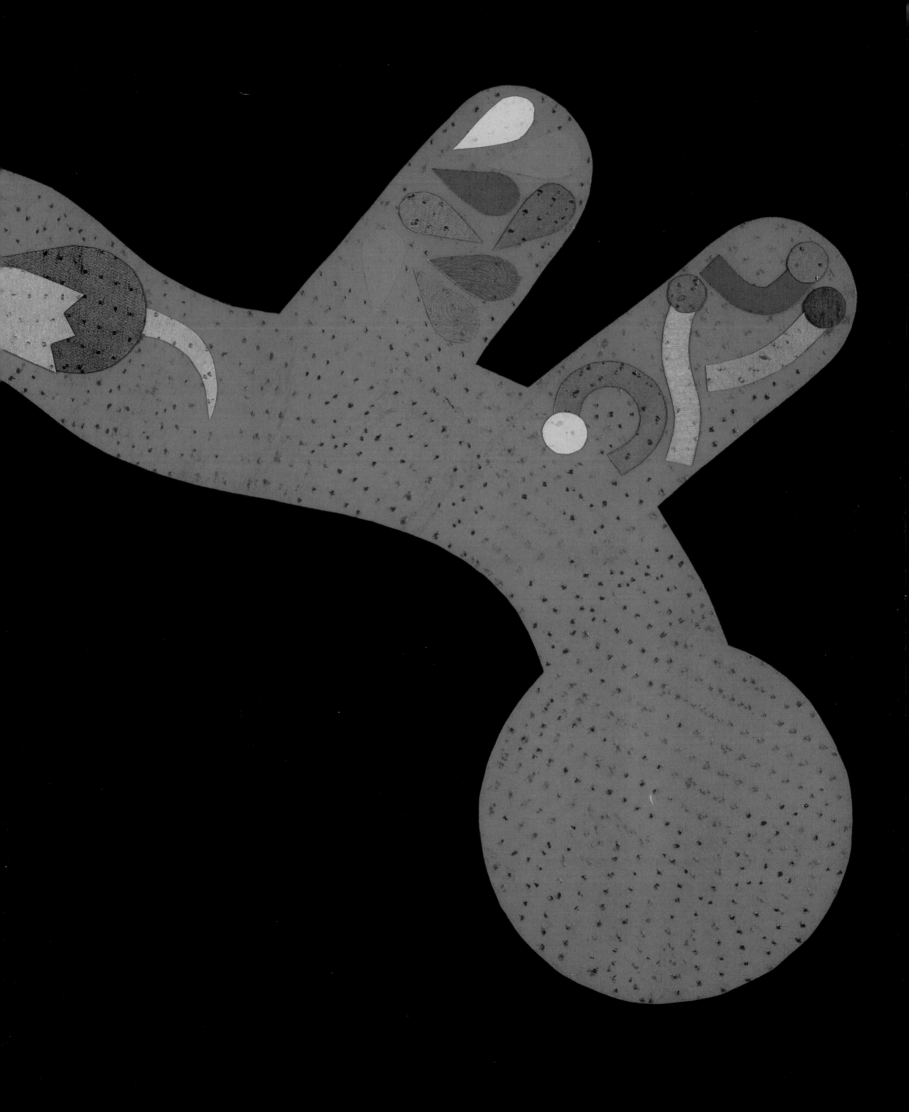

Dear Mole,
Meet us
at the
Fox Skunk

tonight,

maple tree.

Raccoon

When the sun went down,
Mole hurried to the
meeting.

"We're planning a
path to the pond,"
said Fox, "and
your hill is
in our way.
It must go."

"Fox says when the maple leaves turn red and orange, you'll have to move," said Raccoon.

"Better listen to Fox—

he's got

big teeth."

Mole's snout quivered.
This was not good news.

Mole went home. She didn't want to move. She loved her home right where it was.

Suddenly she had an idea.

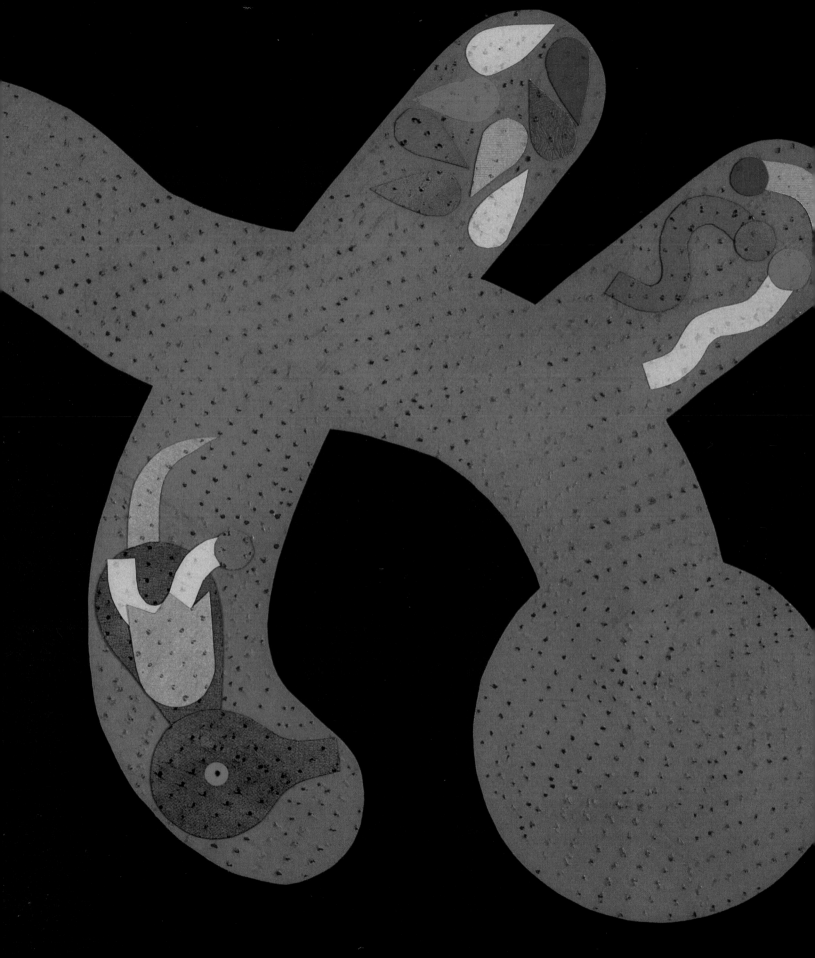

ome days later Raccoon and
kunk strolled by Mole's hill.
t looked bigger. "I wonder
hat that Mole is up to,"
accoon said.

Each night Mole kept digging and digging,
dumping the dirt on top of her hill.

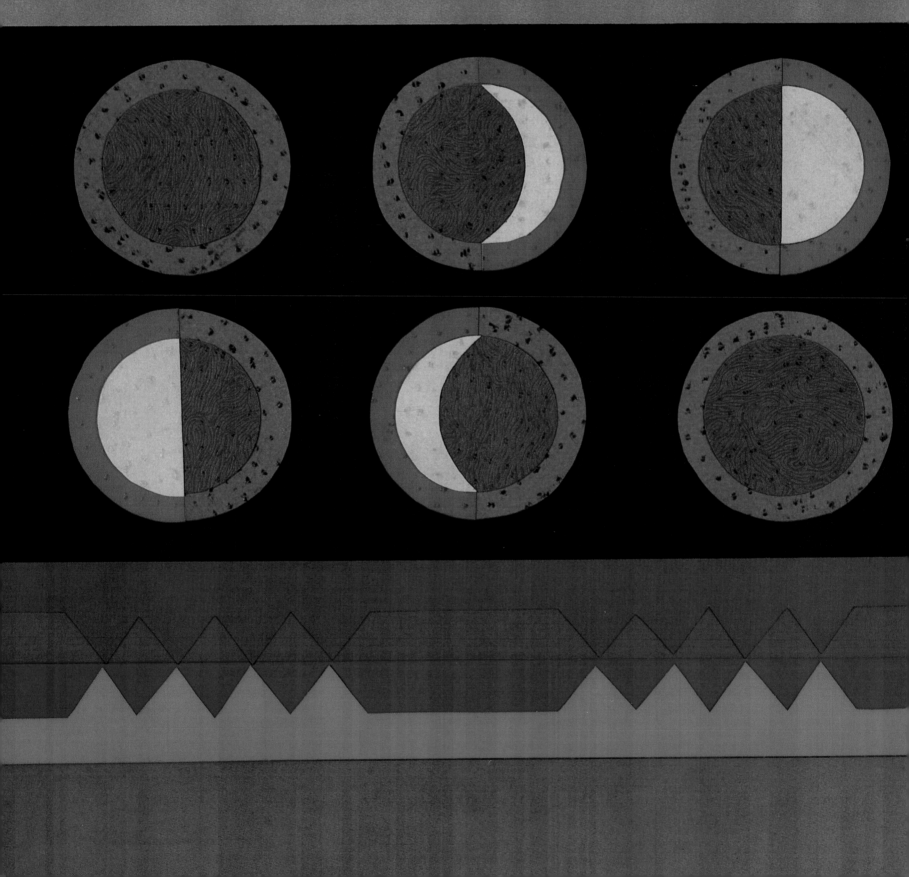

Many moons passed. The hill grew bigger and bigger.
It was time for the next step.

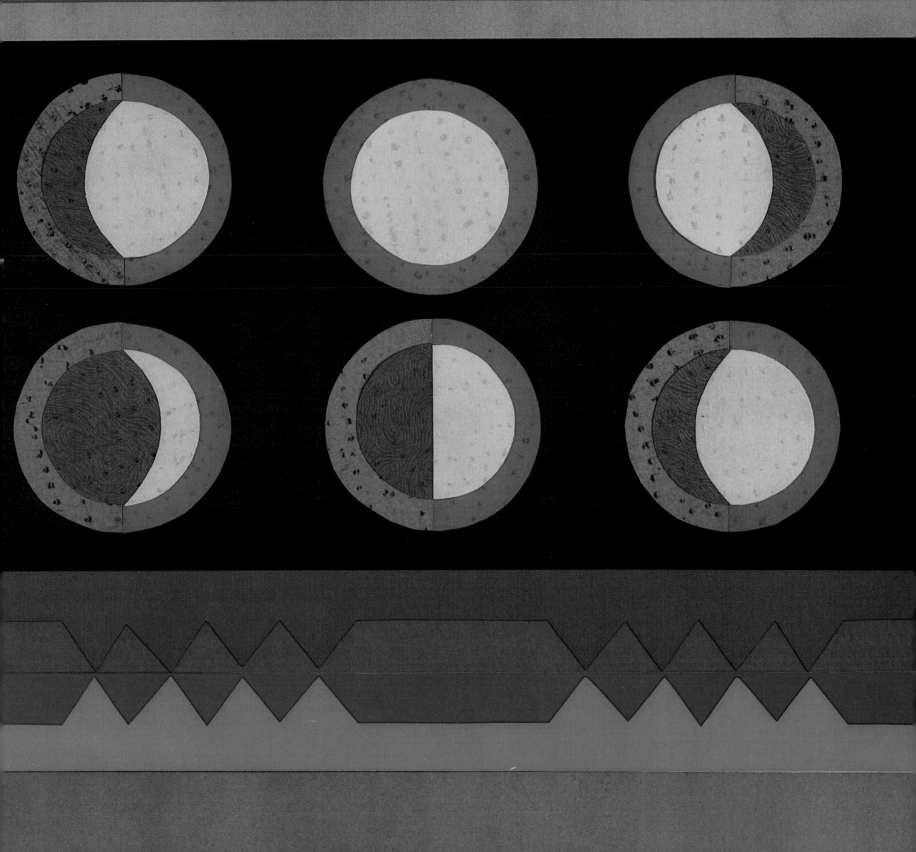

Mole gathered seeds
she had saved
and waited for
the full moon.

She climbed her hill,
planting the seeds
in the dirt as she
went along.

Soon the flower seeds grew up
and burst into bloom.

And the grass seeds inched up
and made a furry carpet.

Mole enjoyed her hill
for the rest of the summer.

Then one day
the maple leaves
turned red and orange.
Just like that,
summer
was over.

Raccoon and Skunk had
forgotten all about Mole.
So when Fox sent them
to see if she had moved,
they were in for
a big surprise.

"What a hill!" said Raccoon.

"What a pickle!" said Skunk.

"If we make Mole move now,

she'll take this great hill with her."

Fox was not going
to believe this.

Of course, he didn't. He had to
see that hill with his own two eyes.
Mole knew he'd come sooner or later.
She was waiting.

Fox circled Mole's hill
on his four furry feet.
"I've been thinking," he said.
"What we need is a tunnel.
Then our path could go
through your hill.
Can you dig it, Mole?"

"I can!"
said Mole.
And she did.

For my brother, Richard Ehlert

The idea for *Mole's Hill* began many years ago with the reading of a Seneca tale called "When Friends Fall Out" included in *American Indian Tales and Legends* by Vladimir Hulpach, translated by George Theiner (Paul Hamlyn, London, 1965). This story evolved from a fragment of that tale.

Mole's Hill is set in the woodlands of Wisconsin. The animals illustrated (fox, skunk, mole, and raccoon) — as well as the plants, flowers, and trees (including jack-in-the-pulpit, lady's slipper, hepatica, morel, trillium, bloodroot, wild asparagus, grape, strawberry, raspberry, and sugar maple) — are all indigenous to the area.

The illustrations were inspired by two art forms of the Woodland Indians: ribbon appliqué and sewn beadwork.

Ribbon appliqué utilizes floral and geometric patterns that are traced onto silk ribbons, cut out, and sewn to clothing such as shirts, blouses, skirts, leggings, moccasins, and borders on blankets and shawls. Beadwork, which is hand-sewn to bags, mittens, shirts, and moccasins, uses motifs from nature such as flowers and leaves.

My thanks to: Milwaukee Public Library and Milwaukee Public Museum, Milwaukee, Wisconsin; Cooperative Children's Book Center, University of Wisconsin-Madison, and Wisconsin State Historical Society, Madison, Wisconsin; The Art Institute of Chicago and Field Museum of Natural History, Chicago, Illinois; The Chandler-Pohrt Collection, Detroit Institute of Arts, Detroit, Michigan; and many private collections.

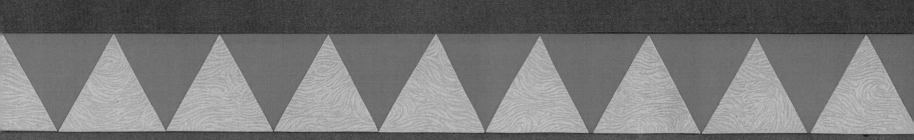

www.hmhco.com

First Voyager Books edition 1998
Voyager Books is a registered trademark of Harcourt, Inc.

MER

4500775114

Printed in the U.S.A.

The Library of Congress has cataloged the hardcover edition as follows:
Ehlert, Lois.
Mole's hill: a woodland tale/Lois Ehlert.
p.   cm.
Summary: When Fox tells Mole she must move to make way for a new path, Mole finds an ingenious way to save her home.
ISBN 978-0-15-255116-2
ISBN 978-0-15-201890-0 pb
[1. Woodland Indians—Legends.   2. Indians of North America—Legends.
3. Moles (Animals)—Folklore]   I. Title.
E78.E2E33   1994
[E]—dc20   93-31151